That Bitch Just Might Be a Vampire

That Bitch Just Might Be a Vampire

Aldadis Trudeau

49 Chambers Publishing, LLC

For more information: hello@49ChambersPublishing.com

http://www.49ChambersPublishing.com

ISBN 979-8-9917472-0-2 (eBook)

ISBN 979-8-9917472-2-6 (Hardcover)

First Edition : October 2024

Contents

Dedication

This book is dedicated to all you slow bitches who can't spot a vampire in your midst.

You're welcome.

Introduction

I want to start by saying I have absolutely nothing against vampires. Real or fake. Although, if I had to deal with a vampire, I'd choose the fake vampires because they pose less of a risk to my life. But that's me.

Humor me and think about your friend group for a minute. All of us have at least one weird ass friend. You know, the one that doesn't quite fit in *anywhere*, but you love her quirky ass anyway? The one who loses all ability to communicate once other humans enter the stratospheric friend bubble or is ready to curse a mufukka out as soon as they approach the friend group. Or there's the one friend who either dresses weird as hell or does entirely too much with the outfit. Bitch! We're going to happy hour; why do you have on an all-black leotard and corset with red bottoms?

Perhaps you have that one friend who takes antisocial to another level. She's the friend who won't commit to an outing to save her life. She says she might show up but rarely does. When she does show up, she's cool as hell, but she's got a shit ton of rules. She says it's because of what she does for a living, but have you ever considered the bitch might be a blood-sucking, nighttime-loving vampire?

Of course, you haven't considered the possibility that vampires are real. You don't know the first thing about vampires except for what you've seen on TV, and that shit is fake, right? Wrong. You're so damn wrong it's scary. Vampires are out here walking among us, late in the evening hours, of course, living it up. They're masquerading as regular-ass people, doing regular-ass shit like making friends, working, taking trips, and complaining about how hard it is to find a good man in this day and age. The whole time they've found at least 39 good men, they've just outlived or killed them all! And look at your dumbass, falling for the okey-doke. The whole time this chic has been showing you who she is, you're just too damn remedial to recognize the signs.

Thankfully, I knew there was a slew of clueless mufukkas walking the streets of America: Chicago, New York, and the Great Lakes, unaware their BFF was really a BSV (blood-sucking vampire). And, please, don't try to correct my geography. Anyone unknowingly hanging out with a vampire is not qualified to tell me that Chicago is in America. There are also some slow mufukkas in South America, Africa, all over Asia, and in the land down under - basically, slow mufukkas on every continent. Put yourself where you fit in. I'm going to go ahead and exclude Antarctica and the poles because of the remarkably low population, which is not ideal for the vampiric food supply. If I'm wrong, sue me (not really). But should you meet a vampire during your travels to the North Pole, tell me so that I can update this guide.

Not so seriously, though, you've got this guide (obviously), and a spark has been lit (hopefully) in your brain. How would you know if your BFF is a vampire? How can you be sure? Is this bitch a real vampire? Is she going to try to turn you into her eternal vampire bestie? Is it feasible to be friends with a vampire without getting "turned" or used for food? What are the signs? What do you do?

Those are all very valid concerns. Unfortunately, I don't have *all* the answers, but I'm willing to share what little wisdom I do have on the subject for the low cost of whatever this book costs. Honestly. Truly. Let's not put a price on your life right now. Instead, let's explore a few signs that you can look out for.

Let's Get Started

Alright! You're here. You've either got one weird-ass friend, or someone thought you were the weird-ass friend that could benefit from this guide. Now would probably be a good time to sit down and have a word with yourself, say a prayer, or practice deep breathing. Then, ask yourself a few vital questions about your BFF.

Is the bitch ashen? Not ashy, but ashen. You can tell she moisturizes, but does she have an odd, murky, clammy color to her skin? It's hard to describe with words. So, if she's of the Caucasian persuasion, does she look like she's never seen a tanning bed? Is the makeup a bit heavy and a shade or two off? Is she giving "Nordic pale," but this bitch claims she's from down south? Or the bitch has melanin in her skin. She is clearly brown but has a slight coat of leftover baby powder embedded in her soul, and it's coming through her pores. It's like a dusty glow that offends you and your home girls because the shit is just unnatural! You know what I'm talking about? And if you don't...pay attention!

What about Sundays? Does she habitually miss Sunday bottomless mimosas? When you question further, does this bitch say she doesn't even like mimosas? Who in the hell doesn't like bottomless mimosas? That is NOT a thing! Has she made any attempt to even meet you at the restaurant *during the day*? You said, "No?" Ok. When she does actually show up for drinks, is it at night? Don't think too hard. We all know the answer. Now, are you noticing how she's never available to meet up during the day? Who doesn't like daylight? Say it with me now...VAMPIRES.

Maybe you're thinking, "No. That can't be. There's a reasonable explanation. She's just different." And I get it. You want to believe your friend is just an oddball. You like her. She's not a bad person, just a little different. Scratch that shit...she's A LOT different. You love an underdog, don't you? Or maybe you don't have a lot of friends. Whatever the reason, it's not entirely your fault. You need a bit more convincing. So, let's do a deeper dive for your slow ass.

Have you ever been to her house? I bet my last $5 that if you have, it's almost always in the evening. I imagine it's tough to get a hold of her during the day. And when you do, I bet she sounds annoyed and sleepy. They let her sleep at the secret government job? When you do get through the door, what do you have to eat? Does she never have food in her refrigerator, but she has bottles of label-less wine she won't share? Is the place dim? Does she have blackout curtains, some new-age electronic blinds, and more curtains on top of that? Why do you think that is? Photosensitivity? No. Uriticaria? Did she tell you that, or have you been looking stuff up online? Get off the internet!

How about the famiglia? Most of us know if our close friends have siblings and have been introduced in some form or fashion. You may not be the closest to their siblings, but at least you know they exist. Some of us have been invited to the annual family cookout, a holiday, or a birthday party and actually showed up. You had a good time! You like them, or you don't. Who cares! You met them, so you know they exist. But have you ever met her family? Not the pale-ashen mufukkas who she runs into while she's out and about at night. Her actual, blood-related family. One parent. Any parent, really. Siblings. Cousins. Play cousins - an aunt or uncle (greats included). Hell, we'll settle for a stepparent, a cousin twice removed, a grandparent in the early stages of dementia, or anyone who grew up with this mysterious vixen. I guarantee you will meet none of the above, around or under.

I bet she has every excuse as to why you haven't met her family. They live out of town or out of the country. She's adopted, and she doesn't get along with her adoptive family. It was a closed adoption. She has no siblings, and her parents are dead. Are they dead or are they UNDEAD?! Her parents were in the military, and they traveled her whole life, so she doesn't really know her family on either side. No matter the excuse, she's got 'em, and you haven't met her family for a good reason. None of the reasons she gave, but...ya girl's family has *been* dead! The only family you're going to meet is the pale-ashy mufukkas that turned her or that she hangs out with. You may not even meet them because they're probably fuckin with her for not having turned y'all or used you for breakfast/lunch/dinner sustenance.

While we're on the topic of sustenance. Have you ever seen this bitch actually eat? When has she ever had a meal with you? When you offer to share your hummus dip, does she say, "Oh, I'm not hungry. You eat it." Let me guess, she's allergic. Have you noticed that she's never hungry? Did the bitch arm start to turn red and burn when you offered her some of your homemade garlic bread? Did she start to gag and back away like you offered her a pile of shit? Did this trick say she was allergic to garlic, too? How many allergies does this chic have? Who the hell is allergic to garlic? I mean, I'm sure plenty of regular people are, but this is not a regular person. Think about it. I guarantee you haven't seen this chic put a bite of food to her lips! I guarantee it!

What about outings? Forget bottomless mimosas for the moment. After avoiding you during the day, is this bitch ready to "turn up" as soon as the sun goes down? When you all meet up for a night out, does she insist on bringing her red wine to events? And only red wine! First off, how in the hell does she get away with that? Secondly, why is it just red wine? Does the bitch refuse to share? Have you ever really paid attention to the wine? Like, really paid attention to the wine in the glass. The shit is thick as fuck! "What kind of wine is this bitch drinking?" you ask yourself. It's not fuckin wine, you dumbass!

What, exactly, does this chic do for work? Does she claim to work in finance or for some super-secret government agency with three letters? Do you even know the name of the agency she works for? Even if it is a three-letter agency, she can at least tell you which one or give you the first two letters. Let's play along and assume she can't tell you, then, what's her job title? Everybody has a title. If the janitor is the "sanitation specialist," then this bitch has to have a damn job title. Has she introduced you to anyone from the job? Does this bitch even have co-workers? Who doesn't have co-workers? Everyone has at least one person they know from work. Why hasn't she invited them to hang out with you and the crew?

And what is her email address? Does this seductress have an email address that sounds a little something like mistress_of_the_night@whoever.com? Or maybe it's nighttimestherighttime666@aol.com. First off, why is this bitch using an antiquated email domain? Do you even know what AOL is? Do you know how old you must be to still have to have an AOL email address? Ancient. Pre-internet. This is a sure sign your bestie is old as fuck! It doesn't matter that she looks 26! She's been 26 for 431 years! She changes with the times, naturally, but not her damn email. That shit stays in the Year of Our Lord 1992. And mistress of the night is a dead-damn-giveaway. If she puts the 6s in her email on purpose...she ain't neva scared. She is not scared of the night, the devil, rottweilers, anything holy, life, gang violence, the mafia, hood people, NOBODY! Do we need to review all the reasons why? There's really just one reason.

Think about all the times y'all have had a night out. When was the last time you were able to take a group picture with her? I'll wait. I'll bet you any money she is never on board to take a picture. While you're ready with the fish lips and peace sign, she ducks out of camera range, grumbling something about the classified government job she can't talk about. They said she can't be on social media, or did they say she can't ever take a picture? Not ever? Does she look so serious that you know not to push the issue any further? Or does she look like she's scared shitless? And for someone who isn't afraid of a lot of shit, being scared to take a picture is a red mufukkin flag! You see where I'm going with this. Of course you do. You're not that damn slow.

Let's say y'all are out having a good ass time, drinking, and not taking group pictures. Maybe you and your other friend go to the bar for more drinks, because y'all don't bring your wine to the club. Or maybe she ran into a friend and walked away to discuss secret vampire shit. Does she know what you and your homegirls were talking about clear across the other side of the club? The bitch doesn't ask what y'all were talking about. She easily slides right into the convo as if she'd been standing there the whole time. You don't question it because that's just how she is. She never misses a beat. Not a detail. Nothing.

You never thought to ask yourself, "How in the lowercase fuck does she know what we're talking about when she's been talking to someone else, across the room, for the past 10 minutes?" I would suspect that your BFF has supersonic vampire bat hearing. I'm not a scientist. I could be wrong, but I'm probably not. That bat echolocation comes in handy for her ass. Did you know some scientists say that female bats may have a higher sensitivity to sound? I'm just saying. Maybe you stop making excuses and listen to the one possible scientific fact I've given. Or not. I'm not done, though.

—◦✦◦—

Now, considering all the things she won't do, sometimes she'll pick you up. She'll even drive y'all to wherever y'all are headed. It's rare, but she does it. Think about this bitch car. Does she have illegal tint on her car windows, and no matter how often she gets pulled over, she refuses to take that shit off? Is it like riding in a damn coffin? Is her car black? Is the interior black? It doesn't have to be, but eight times out of 10, that shit is black as hell.

It's nice that she'll drive sometimes but do you and your friends really want to ride with her? Is she the ride of last resort because she has way too many damn rules? Y'all have to leave the club at a certain time if she's driving, right? She's probably threatened to leave you hoes at the club if you don't head to the parking lot at 4:04 am. Does she have a thousand reasons why she can't go to happy hour but will pick y'all up to head to the club as soon as night falls? Is she going to review the departure, arrival, and parking lot pick-up times with y'all before she starts the car? I Thought so.

—◦✦◦—

You've invited her on at least two girls' trips each year since you've known her. What's that like? Let me see if I can guess. She comes up with reason after reason not to travel more than 4 hours away, so going out of the country is an automatic "hell no!" She'll consider coming on the trip but can only travel at night because of work. She lets you know, off the bat, that she's not sharing a room with anyone. If she can come, she will definitely be working during the day, so that she won't be available for any daytime activities.

I hear some of you saying you weren't paying attention to any of this or none of it applies. Okay. Okay. Try inviting her on a girl's trip (real or make-believe). If she pauses, her eyes start darting around, and the left eye squints, followed by a long sigh. Just know you are witnessing this bitch's wheels spinning in her mind, trying to calculate the miles and time to travel, plus the total number of hours of daylight divided by sunset and sunrise times. Whatever the outcome…I told you so.

So, she doesn't come on the trip. No big deal. She's a hardworking professional with a very important government job that no one knows the name of. She's still your bestie. She's reliable. You can talk to her about anything. She's always there for you. It's just hard to get a hold of her during the day. But if you have relationship issues, she will always listen.

Ever notice how she is really invested in knowing about your relationships? Of course, you haven't because she's your BFF, and she wouldn't be your bestie if she weren't ready to hear about the shit that goes on in your relationships. If you're single or dating, think about the last few guys you dated. Think about the ones that cheated or were the equivalent of 16 red flags and four bottles of antipsychotics. When you told your BFF, did she get pissed, pace the floors cursing, threatened to kick his ass, but calmed down, came back to the couch, and told you it was going to be ok? Of course, she did. She's supportive. Right! Now think about where those sorry bastards are now.

Do the men that do you wrong come up missing or stop responding? Were any of their cars found abandoned at the airport parking lot, in swamp water, or not at all? Did you check their social media to see who this sorry POS is dating after ghosting the shit out of you, and there are no updates? No recent activity. No pictures of him out with his friends on their pages? Are there no new pages? Interesting! Is it like the mufukkas just disappeared from the living world? Girl! What happened to them? Are these mufukkas DEAD? Did you tell your homegirl about that shit just a few nights ago? Did y'all recently have a come to Joshua (we're not about to play with the Lord today) about your poor choice in men? Did she ask you to leave them alone? Please don't call, text, or reach out to them on social media...for a while. She said you needed to heal, huh? Crazy. It's like you gave her gift cards to her favorite restaurant. The way I see it, this bitch is a vampire or a serial killer. Neither one of those is good, but if I had a choice, I'd hope she was a vampire.

—◈◆◈—

I know it's an unusual question, but what do you call her? As you know, her government name is LaShauna, Kellie, Michelle, or Tanya. Does this diva want people to call her Mistress Lashauna or Mistress Tanya? At first, you thought this shit was a joke. Like, where did that shit come from? You and your friends are asking each other, "Who does this bitch think she is? Mistress who?" And I'm not talking streetwalker, lady of the night, type mistress. I'm damn sure not talking, whips, chains, and leather unitards Mistress, either. Well, come to think of it....she may very well be into the dominatrix scene. What better way to find easy victims? They trust her to tie them up and do some kinky shit. And she is happy to oblige before she drinks their blood, hoe! You may be on the slow side, but your BSV bestie might be a mufukkin genius.

Have you found yourself wondering why she's always so damn close to you? Like, she's always sniffing you, talking about, "Damn, friend! You smell good!" While your brain freezes trying to run a mental check to see if you put on deodorant, let alone perfume, this bitch is literally smelling you. You may have never questioned her sexuality before this, but you're noticing just how close the bitch mouth is to your neck.

Meanwhile, your brain comes back online, and you determine you definitely put on deodorant but not the perfume. So, why is this trick so close to you? Why is she still smelling your damn neck? Because she's smelling the O-positive blood coursing through your carotid artery! You smell like a mufukkin snack!

Shit You Can Do

Hopefully, at this point, you're realizing you really don't know much about your BFF. The bitch is shrouded in mystery and believable excuses. If you're still in denial and making excuses for her...bless your little slow-ass heart! I know it's hard to believe, but this bitch just might be a vampire.

At this point, you may be wondering what to do. Your brain has come up with a thousand-and-one scenarios, and you are literally about to lose your shit. Perhaps you're considering confronting her. You ask yourself if you should coordinate a "bitch are you a vampire?" intervention with your friends. The thought of consuming more garlic and investing in some holy water is at the forefront of your reasoning. Are you searching Joe Biden's internet for holy water? Is that a rabbit hole you really want to go down? If you've ever seen a vampire movie, you know that vampires move at the speed of light, so I would NOT suggest confronting the BSV bestie in person. Any intervention, no matter how well thought out, may end up in your demise. Would you confront a serial killer? If you said "yes," please take your ass to counseling immediately! There is obviously something wrong with your decision-making skills. Seek help.

I know. I know. Here I am, disrupting your weird but happy little friendship and making you question your bestie with not one solution on how to handle this shit. Have no fear; a few action steps are here. I don't know if I would call them "solutions" because that would imply that I'm telling you how to fix something. Honestly. Truly. I don't know that having a vampire bestie is necessarily a fixable problem. You may not even consider it a problem. So, what I offer instead are a few different approaches to help you navigate a friendship with your vampire bestie.

In the event that you decide you don't want to be friends with your vampire ex-bestie, can we please, please agree that you will not try to put a wooden stake through her heart? Whether the chic is dead or not, that's still murder, and I don't even know what kind of time you're looking at for vampire murder. Will there be a body, or will it burst into ashes like the movies? Hell, I don't know, and I'm not trying to find out. And hopefully, neither are you. If you are, put this down and locate a counselor immediately cause something ain't right with you. Otherwise, let's get into it.

Show your acceptance without coming out and saying, "Bitch! I know you're a vampire!" Chances are your dumbass is going to die shortly afterward. Perhaps you should consider scheduling your next outing with her specific vampiric needs in mind. Invite her to meet up at your place before heading out. Make sure she knows you'll be leaving with enough time to get her home before sunrise. You know that mirror by your front door, the one she always avoids? Cover it! Or remove it altogether and replace it with one of those "Home Starts with Us" or "Welcome to Mi Casa!" signs. Believe me, she will notice it's gone. She's been creatively ducking and dodging that damn mirror since she met you. Once it's gone, her vampirey senses will start twitching, and that bitch'll be paying close attention to your next moves.

You know she's coming with her bottle of wine. No need to feel so comfortable as to say, "Bitch, I know you over there drinking blood in that wine bottle!" Are you trying to die? No? Ok, good. Invest in a few dark-colored or solid-colored wine glasses, and make sure you have them out for her when she comes. This way, she can drink her fake ass wine-blood incognito. Hopefully, she'll get a good sense that you know and accept her.

Use subtle protection even if you're not afraid of becoming vampire food. By subtle, I mean keeping something protective on or around you, *just in case*. You don't have to wear a big-ass Jesus piece on a thick-ass rope chain. That is the exact OPPOSITE of subtle. Think about investing in a silver necklace you wear *under* your clothes. Maybe a few silver earrings and rings would make it seem more like "a look" rather than a security measure. Don't go ordering random silver jewelry from the interwebs! Make sure the shit is real; otherwise, it's pointless, and yo ass is dead. That means you look for the 925 on the sterling silver.

Let's say you're able to get your hands on a good bit of holy water. Sure, you can keep it in a silver flask in your purse because that's subtle as hell. Or you can get one of those travel-size spray bottles. You know, when you're flying, they're the ones that hold three fl. oz. of liquid so you can put it in your carry-on or purse? Yeah? That one. Fill that bad boy up with your holy water and have it on hand. Could be tequila! It could be holy water! Who knows! You never know when you have to spray a blood-sucking bitch down or need a quick spritz of liquid courage. But if it's tequila...make sure you don't use it instead of the holy water. Maybe you put the tequila in the flask instead. You know your ass is kinda slow. We don't need you getting confused, spraying that hoe with liquor, and then her figuring out your plan and using your neck like a Slurpee.

—◦✦◦—

Start taking garlic supplements. You would need to ease into this one. That means you start by saying a bit about how your head has been hurting and your vision has been a bit blurry. You might even make a stink about how you think your blood pressure has been high, but you're too young to have "the pressure." Then you want to start sharing little tidbits about how you're waiting for a doctor's appointment and how long it's taking. Of course, your friends will be supportive and offer advice, like what their grandmas took to manage their blood pressure. Blah, blah, blah! I guarantee one of them says their grandparents took garlic pills, and you ponder the thought and tell them you think it's a good idea and you'll try anything at this point.

So, while you're waiting for the doctor's appointment, you're going all in on trying holistic shit. You officially love herbs 'n shit! Then, you start your garlic supplements. This way, if your pores are emitting the smell of hot garlic, it doesn't seem out of place and throw your homegirl into a fit of vampirey fuckery that leads to the end of your life.

It is important to note that your vampiric bestie is not a damn fool! The bitch can literally hear your blood coursing through your veins. She knows if your blood pressure is high because it sounds like the chorus to "Bohemian Rhapsody" in her ears. If she's hearing elevator music humming through your regular pressure veins, she's going to be on high alert. So, bitch, be prepared! Maybe your blood pressure only bothers you after lunch or when you've been sitting for a while. I don't know how the shit works. I don't have high blood pressure! I'm not a medical professional, but I do know you're probably looking to have a funky ass stroke if the top number is 180 or higher and the bottom number is over 120. Let's not have stroke-level blood pressure, ok? Get on Joe Biden's internet and look up symptoms, how to take your blood pressure, and learn all about your fake ass medical condition. Hell! You may actually have high blood pressure after finding out this bitch is a vampire and the lengths you have to go to protect your neck! But, for the love of all that's good, BITCH, please do your damn research!

While I'm sure there are a gazillion other pointers I could provide, bitch I'm tired of thinking for all of us. I can't be the only one trying to save your raggedy ass. It's important that you are actively trying to save your own raggedy ass if you're going to continue running the streets of America with your blood-hungry homegirl. I've got nothing but love for you, baby, but that's all I've got for you hoes.

In Conclusion

If you've found any of this information helpful, entertaining, or dumb as hell, please share it with a friend. And by share, I mean purchase it and give it to another slow-ass friend who may have befriended a vampire or who needs a good laugh. After all, sharing is supposed to be caring, although I don't think that holds to the sharing of sexually transmitted infections. I digress! That is a guide for another group of slow mufukkas.

Thank you for reading any part of this guide and, most importantly, for your support. Befriend vampires responsibly; you slow hoe!

About the Author

Aladis Trudeau is a modern-day philosopher and renaissance woman who whiles away her hours planning for the future of humanity. She is dedicated to providing common sense approaches to problems such as a vampire epidemic, a zombie apocalypse and alien invasions.

Sign up for our newsletter to stay updated on the next installment of the "That Bitch Just Might Be..." series, being released in Spring 2025.

http://www.49chamberspublishing.com

www.ingramcontent.com/pod-product-compliance
Lightning Source LLC
Chambersburg PA
CBHW071446300726
48976CB00004B/1451